The Berenstain Bears' ®

HOME SWEET TREE

Stan & Jan Berenstain

sourcebooks
jabberwocky

Hello, friends.
This way, please.
Just ahead,
just past these trees,
is our home,
our Home Sweet Tree.
Home sweet, home sweet,
Home Sweet Tree!

Our tree stands tall,
fine, fat, and round.
Its roots dig deep
into the ground.

Come on in!
Up we go!
There's a lot
for us to show!

Look! Look!
Over there!
You know him.
It's Papa Bear,
snoozing in
his easy chair.

Papa always
takes a snooze
while looking at
the TV news.

Look! Look!
Look in there!
You know her.
It's Mama Bear.

Our mom's a super
cookie maker,
a chocolate chip
cookie baker!

Yum! Yum!
Let's have some!

Join us, friends.
Come, and we
will all eat cookies
in our Home Sweet Tree.

Come! Come!
Come with me.
There's more to see
in our Home Sweet Tree!

Come and look.
Look if you dare.
The cellar
of our home's
down there.

The light we shine
will show the way
and chase the spooky
dark away.

This is the place
where we store
what we don't need
anymore.

Toys and things
that we've outgrown—
cradle, crib,
baby's bib,
bottles, blocks,
toy telephone.

But there is much,
much more to see.
Come on, friends!
Follow me!

All the way
to the top of our tree,
our home sweet, home sweet,
Home Sweet Tree.

To the special
room I share
with my brother,
Brother Bear.

My things
are here.
My brother's things
are over there.

My closet's neat.
I must confess…

my brother's closet
is a mess!

You've seen our home
inside and out.
Home is what
we're all about.

Good-bye, friends!
Please come again.
But will you also
tell us when...

When we can see
your Home Sweet Tree?
Home sweet, home sweet,
Home Sweet Tree!

Published by Sourcebooks Jabberwocky, an imprint of Sourcebooks, Inc.
P.O. Box 4410, Naperville, Illinois 60567-4410
(630) 961-3900
Fax: (630) 961-2168
www.jabberwockykids.com

Originally published in the United States of America by Golden Books.

Library of Congress Cataloging-in-Publication data is on file with the publisher.

Source of Production: Leo Paper, Heshan City, Guangdong Province, China
Date of Production: June 2013
Run Number: 20382

Printed and bound in China
LEO 10 9 8 7 6 5 4 3 2 1